Disney · PIXAR
FINDING
NEMO JOKE
BOOK

PUFFIN BOOKS

PUFFIN BOOKS

Published by the Penguin Book Group

Penguin Books Australia Ltd
250 Camberwell Road
Camberwell, Victoria 3124, Australia

First published in Australia by Penguin Books Australia, 2003

2003 © Disney Enterprises, Inc./Pixar Animation Studios

Written by Ben Hampson, Allan Daldy, Ben Mellonie, Roderick Potts, Joanne Lomasney
Cover design by Steve Williams, text design by Ben Rydz
Printed and bound in Australia by McPherson's Printing Group, Maryborough, Victoria

10 9 8 7 6 5 4 3 2
ISBN 0 14 330088 1

Disney · PIXAR
FINDING
NEMO JOKE
BOOK

Written by

Ben 'Clown Fish' Hampson
Allan 'Jet Stream' Daldy
Roderick 'Barrier Reef' Potts
Ben 'Tiger shark' Mellonie
Joanne 'Sea Star' Lomasney

PUFFIN BOOKS

What do you call a fish with no eyes?

Fsh!

What did Marlin's doctor
do when he couldn't
make Marlin feel better?

He sent him
to a sturgeon!

Which fish love
it when the sea
freezes over?

Skates!

UNDERSEA CELEBRITIES

Sharkira
Mussel Crowe
Sea-anu Reeves
Nafin Buckley
Kylie Minnow
Gill Smith
Justin Timberflake
Leonardo Di Carprio
Jelly Osbourne
Sarah My-Shell Gellar
Crab Pitt

Where will Nemo go to
complete his education?

FINishing school!

Which fish hangs in the
sky and shines at night?

A moonfish!

Why did Dory take hours to make a decision?

She wanted to mullet over!

Which fish has a halo and wings?

An angelfish!

Why couldn't Marlin afford a new house?

Cause he didn't have anemone!

Why did the flounder
go to the doctor?

Cause he was feeling
a bit flat!

Why was Old King Cole
like a happy fish?

Cause he was a
merry old sole!

Which fish has the
deepest voice?

A sea bass!

What is Gill's
favourite game?

Name that tuna!

What fish travels at
100 kilometres per hour?

A motor pike!

What do
fish like
to chew?

Bubble gum!

What's a whale's favourite game?

Swallow the leader!

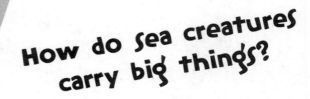

How do sea creatures carry big things?

In a whalebarrow!

What did the hake say
to his naughty son?

For goodness hake!

Why are dolphins
smarter than humans?

They can train
humans to stand at
the side of the pool
and feed them fish!

Where did Mr. Ray find his job?

In the 'kelp wanted' adverts!

Did you hear about the athletic fish who swam round and round the island?

He **lapped** the shore!

Who is the saddest
creature in the sea?

The blue whale!

Why was the
sand wet?

Because the
sea weed!

Why are seabirds easy to fool?

Because they're gull-ible!

How does the sea say goodbye?

With a **wave!**

What did Dory
say to the scary
anglerfish?

Glow away!

What do you get from
a bad-tempered shark?

As far away as possible!

Why does Anchor like head-banging at rock concerts?

Cause he's a hammerhead shark!

Who is the meanest
creature in the sea?
Billy the Squid!

Why did the whale
cross the sea?

To get to the
other **tide!**

What is the eel's
favourite dance?

The conger.

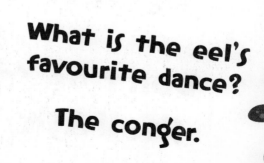

Why wouldn't the fishing boat make it back to shore?

Cause it was too tide!

What did the one hermit crab say to the other hermit crab when he stole his home?

Don't be so shellfish!

What part of a fish weighs the most?

Its scales!

Where do jellyfish sleep on camping holidays?

In **tent**acles!

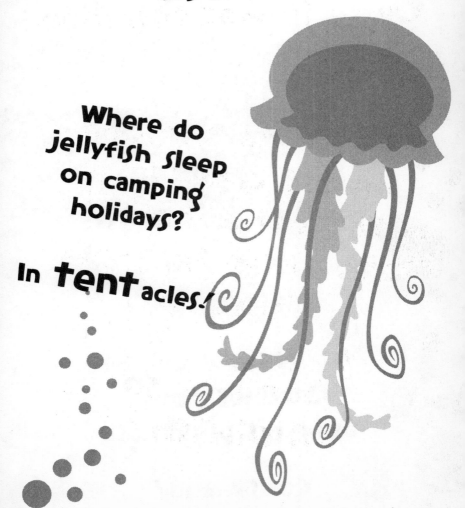

What happens to Bloat
if you make him angry?

He blows up, mate!

What does
Jacques pour
over his puddings?

Cousteaud!

What is the best
way to communicate
with a fish?

Drop it a line!

What do you call
someone who scoops up
lots of fish in one go?

Annette!

Why didn't the sailor's radio work when the sea was rough?

It was on the wrong WAVElength!

Did you hear about the new seafood diet?

You see food and eat it!

What did the underwater cop say about the barracuda's dodgy deal?

That smells fishy!

What did the
photographer
use to take
underwater
pictures?

A fish-eye lens!

Did you hear the one about the fisherman who fell in love with the beautiful fish?

She was a good catch!

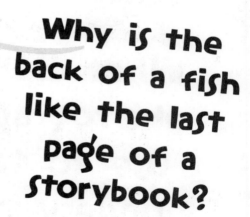

Why is the back of a fish like the last page of a storybook?

They're both the end of a tail!

What do you wear to
an undersea wedding?

A wet suit!

How did the fish feel
when he was sold to
the fishmonger?

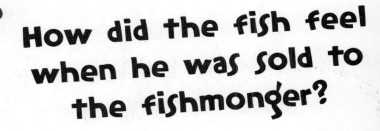

He was gutted!

What do fish
watch in the evening?

Tele**fish**on.

What did Dory say to Marlin?
'Tangs for the memories!'

How do you rate Nemo's
bravery, from one to ten?

He's off the scale!

What happens to sleepy fish at the edge of the reef?

They Drop-off!

What happened when
Dory admitted to
taking the bait?

She was let
off the hook!

LIMERICKS

When Nemo went to school
He thought he'd feel like a fool
'Cos he had a fin
A little too thin.
But in fact ... he's incredibly cool!

In an instant, the deed was done;
Poor Marlin had lost a son.
Determined he was
To find him because
His family was reduced to ... one!

There once was a tang called Dory
Who had a short term mem-ory.
When asked why this was
She said, 'It's because ...'
And couldn't remember the story!

The tank was really dank
The aquarium really stank.
The dentist wasn't mean-
He just tried to clean.
Now Nemo's stuck in the tank.

If you're swimming and see some ships,
It is best to remember these tips:
Stay clear of the net.
Swim fast as a jet.
Or else you'll end up with chips!

There once was a shark named Bruce,
Who decided to call a truce.
He resolved that fish
Were no longer a dish,
And instead, tried vegetable mousse.

What is the **biggest** threat to a coral garden?

Sea weeds!

What's Bruce's favourite beach snack?

Vego Sandwiches!

Where do sea horses live?

In the corral!

What do you get
when you cross
a squid with
an octopus?

A lot of legs, mate!

What did the beach
ask the tide?

'Why are you always going
out without me?'

What undersea creature has no money?

A poor-poise!

Where do king crabs live?

In sand castles!

Where do slimming whales get their weight measured?

At a whale-weigh station!

UNDERSEA JOBS

Piano Tuna
Mini Crab Driver
Carp Park Attendant
Prawnbroker
Loan Shark

How do you make
an undersea trifle?

Get some sea sponges;
add some **jellyfish**;
and mix with currents!

Why was Jacques so patriotic?

He was prawn on the fourth of July!

Whose job is it to keep the reef clean?

The **sea sponge**, of course!

What is Nigel's favourite dance?

The **Peli-can-can!**

What do you get when you cross an aquarium with a computer?

Fish and chips!

What game do fish always avoid?

Netball!

**Who is the greatest
rock 'n' roll band in the ocean?**

The Rolling Stonefish!

What do you call a lobster that bites your backside? A **bottom** feeder!

How do crabs avoid danger? By **sidestepping!**

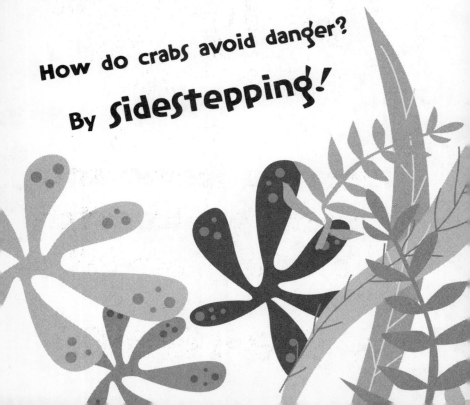

Where do Nemo and his mates go to catch the latest movie?

The *Sea-nema!*

Where do Mr. Ray's students go to borrow books?

The Continental Shelf!

What do **dogfish** do in their spare time?

Chase **catfish**, of course!

What did Gil say when he was taken to an aquarium?

'Tanks for nothing!'

What's the difference between a fish and a piano?

You can't tuna fish!

What is a crustacean's
favourite fruit?

The crab apple!

Which sea creatures come
calling at Christmas time?

Coral singers!

Why are fish
so smart?

Cause they're
always in schools!

What do great white sharks eat?

Anything they want!

Why did Nigel do something he didn't want to do?

Because of **pier** pressure!

Who is the funniest
fish in the sea?

Marlin, of course.
He's a big clown fish!

Who is the coolest
inhabitant of a reef?

The sea fan!

FISHY FRIENDS

What fish is a pirate's best friend?

A parrot fish!

Why is it difficult to make friends with shellfish?

Cause they clam up just as you're getting to know them!

What fish is a
millionaire's best friend?
A gold fish!

What kind of fish is a
carpenter's best friend?
A saw fish!

What fish
is a general's
best friend?
A soldier fish!

Knock Knock Jokes

Knock Knock.
Who's there?
Tide.
Tide who?
Tidy your bedroom!

Knock Knock.
Who's there?
Cod.
Cod who?
Cod ya red-handed!

Dory: Knock Knock.
Marlin: Who's there?
Dory: Er ... I can't remember!

Bernie: Knock knock.
Baz: Who's there?
Bernie: Sue.
Baz: Sue who?
Bernie: Sue-wage pipe!

Knock Knock.
Who's there?
Dooya.
Dooya who?
Dooya know the
way to the EAC?

Knock knock.
Who's there?
Ann.
Ann who?
Ann-chovy.

Knock knock.
Who's there?
Who's a Fred.
Who's a Fred who?
Who's a Fred of sharks?!

What's Crush's favourite drink? Squash!

What do you call dried fruit from Sydney?

East Australian Currants!

UNDERSEA BLOCKBUSTERS

Marlin Rouge

Lord of the Blue-Ringed Octopus

Starfish Wars

Jurassic Carp

Behind Anemone Lines

Marine Poppins

Austin Flounders

Charlie's Angelfish